armor

army

 axe

 baby

baby Jesus

basket

---

children

 city

cloud

  coat

cow

  cross

---

 drink

 ear

eat

 Egypt

 eyes

 feet

 fire

---

 garden

 giant

 girl

go

 ground

 hair

 hand

happy

---

 jail

 jar

 Jesus

 king

 light

 lion

 love

---

 night

 people

 Pharaoh

 pigs

 pray

 queen

 rain

---

 servant

 sheep

 shepherd

 sick

 sing

 snake

 staff

---

 sun

 sword

 table

 temple

 tent

tomb

 tower

---

 water

 wind

 window

 woman

 world

 worship

 wrong

Presented to

_____

By _____

On _____

Amazing Stories of the Bible

A Picture That! Story Bible

Written by
Tracy Harrast

Illustrated by
Garry Colby

Amazing Stories of the Bible

A
Picture That!
Story Bible

Zonder**kidz**

Zonder**kidz**™

The children's group of Zondervan

www.zonderkidz.com

Amazing Stories of the Bible
Copyright © 2002 by Tracy Harrast
Illustrations copyright © 2002 by Garry Colby

Requests for information should be addressed to:
Zonderkidz, *Grand Rapids, Michigan 49530*

ISBN: 0-310-70218-6

Editor: Gwen Ellis
Interior Design: Jody DeNeef and Todd Sprague
Art Direction: Michelle Lenger

Printed in China

04 05 06 /❖HK/ 10 9 8 7 6 5 4 3

A Note to Moms & Dads

When I was five or six years old, I informed my mother: "I don't need to go to Sunday school anymore because I've already heard all of the Bible stories." I'm glad she kept taking me because, obviously, the Bible held much more to discover! This book tells many Bible stories that are amazing.

The little pictures within the text of this book not only add fun, they make reading easy for beginners. The first time my five-year-old son, Ryan, ever read a complete sentence was when he picked up from my desk the manuscript for my first storybook of this kind—*Picture That! Bible Storybook*. He beamed and said, "Hey, I can read this! I can read this!" I was thrilled to hear him sound out the simple words. Every time he came to a picture within the text, he smiled because he could guess the word it represented. The pictures in the sentences gave him the hints he needed for reading by himself.

I hope you'll feel the same joy as you hear your children read aloud these amazing stories simplified from God's Holy Word. It is my prayer that as you read together, you and your children will be awed by God's power and touched by his love.

Tracy L. Harrast

Dedication

To my 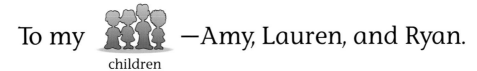 —Amy, Lauren, and Ryan.

I love you and I am happy that you walk

in the light.

Table of Contents

Old Testament

Oh No! Sin Comes In 2

The First Rainbow 4

A Tower to Heaven 6

Angels Come to Lunch 8

A Woman Becomes Salt 10

A Mean Wedding Trick 12

Joseph's Strange Dreams 14

Moses Sees God's Glory 16

A Holdup Wins a Battle 18

A House for God 20

A Talking Donkey 22

A Spy Mission 24

You Want to Go Where? 26

Just Look and Live 28

Aaron's Staff Blooms 30

An Ark That Wasn't a Boat 32

Joshua's Amazing Battles 34

The Moldy Bread Trick 36

Amazing Deborah Wins a War 38

Surprising Signs for Gideon 40

The Incredible Shrinking Army 42

Samuel Picks the Little Guy 44

Saul's Close Calls 46

David Helps a Lame Guy 48

Who's the Real Mom? 50

The Incredible Expanding Food 52

Fire Falls from Heaven 54

Three Thirsty Kings 56

The Miraculous Oil Jar 58

An Axe Head Floats 60

Chariots of Fire to the Rescue 62

An Eight-Year-Old King 64

A Shadow Creeps Backward 66

A Praying Queen Foils a Plot 68

It Couldn't Get Much Worse 70

New Testament

Christmas Angels 74

God Speaks Up for His Son 76

Jesus Heals Ten Men at Once 78

Back to Life 80

Jesus—A Good Friend to Bad People 82

Love Your Enemies 84

What Is Most Valuable 86

How Many Hairs Do You Have? 88

Peter Starts to Walk by Faith 90

Runaway Pigs 92

A Fish Delivers a Coin 94

Jesus Puts Back an Ear 96

The Day Jesus Died 98

Jesus Appears 100

The Sewing Lady Comes Back 102

Two Liars Drop Dead 104

Angel Power Opens a Gate 106

Philip Disappears! 108

Stephen Sees Right into Heaven 110

A Clever Escape 112

An Earthquake Shakes the Jail 114

Falling Out the Window 116

Shipwrecked! 118

What's Biting You? 120

God's Amazing Grace 122

Dressed in Armor 124

We're the Body of Christ 126

We're Going Up in the Air 128

Subject Index 130

Who Is Jesus? 135

Old Testament

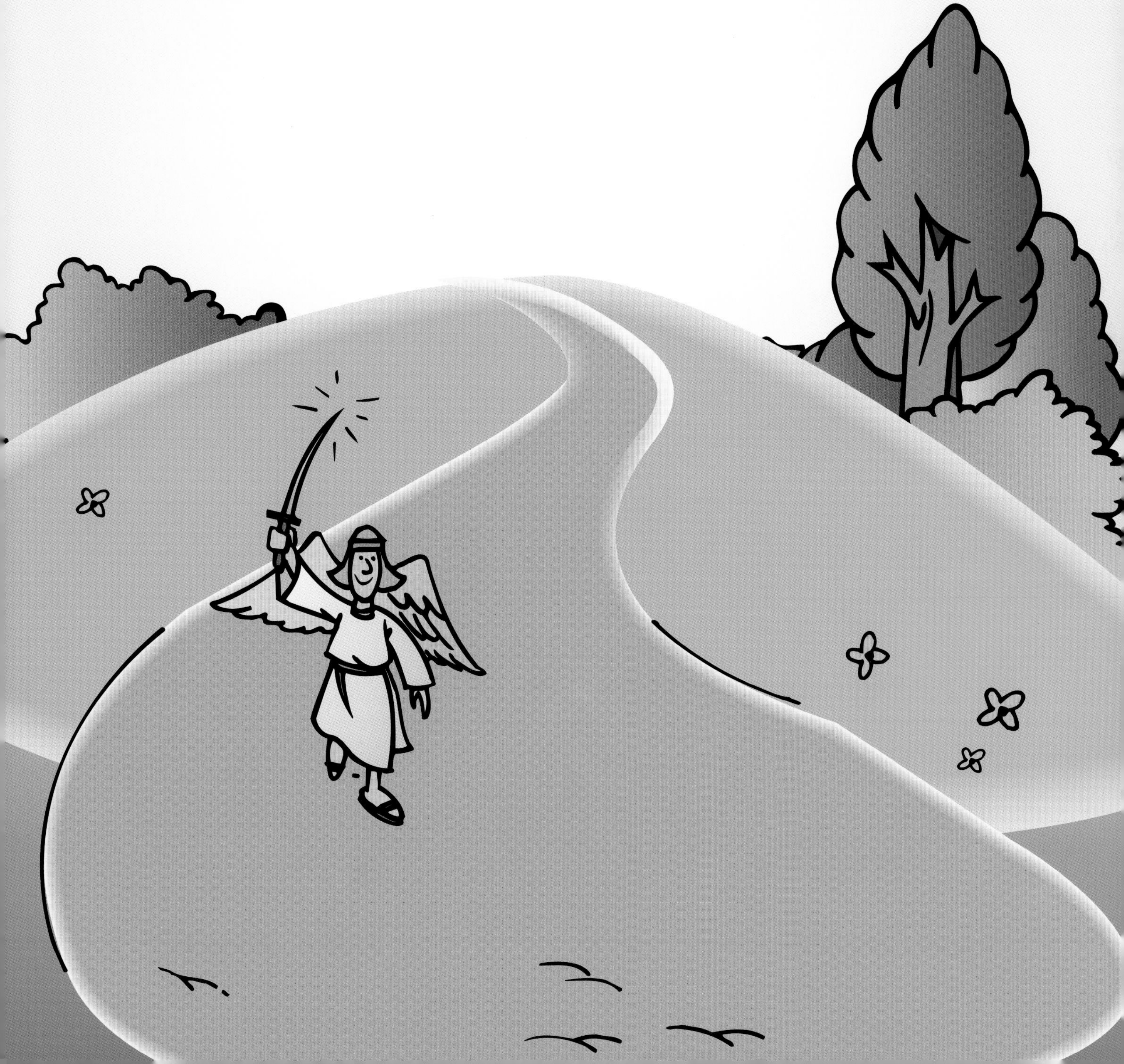

God made the and everything in it. The 1st
world

 God made were Adam and Eve. God said
people

they could any in the of Eden
eat fruit Garden

except **1**. Adam and Eve made the choice. That
wrong

1st sin changed the whole ! Adam and Eve had
world

to leave the . After that, would die and
garden people

have big problems. Many years later God would send

his Son to save from sin and death.
Jesus people

When we believe Jesus died on the cross to take the

punishment for our sins, God will forgive us and will

let us live forever in  heaven with him.

What Did You Learn?

Because Adam sinned, people die. Because Jesus gave his life, people can live forever.

The First Rainbow

Genesis 6:5—8:17

After awhile, in the became so bad

people   world

that *every* thought they had was evil. God was very

. But there was **1** , Noah, who followed God.

sad   man

God told Noah to build a big . Then God sent

ark

at least 2 of every into the . After that,

animal   ark

it so much that covered the .

rained   water   earth

But God kept Noah, his family, and the safe

animals

in the . God promised that it would never

ark

 that much again. He put a rainbow in the

rain

sky as a reminder of his promise.

What Did You Learn?

Rainbows remind us that
God promised not to cover the
whole world with water again.

 A Tower to Heaven

Genesis 11:1-9

When people first lived on the everything
earth

was new, all spoke the same language. When
people

they learned to make bricks, they became proud.

They tried to build a that would reach to
tower **up**

. God did not want them to build the .
heaven **tower**

To them, he changed their languages. They
stop

could not understand each other. So the building

came to a . When a babbles, no one
stop **baby**

6

understands him. No one understood the people

when they talked, so they called the

city

Babel.

What Did You Learn?

God wants us
to be humble.

Angels Come to Lunch

Genesis 18:1-15; 21:1-2

The Lord and **2** angels visited a 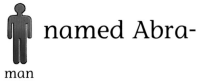 man named Abra-

ham. Abraham told his wife, Sarah, "Quick! Bake

some bread !" He gave his servant a cow to fix

for lunch. The  angels ate the food. Then the

 angels told Abraham a secret. Sarah would

have a baby within **1** year. Sarah laughed. She

thought she was too old to have a baby . The Lord

said, "Is anything too hard for God?" Sarah had the

 at the very time that the Lord had said.

baby

What Did You Learn?

Nothing is too hard for God.

A Woman Becomes Salt

Genesis 18:16—19:26

 People in the city of Sodom and the city of

Gomorrah did wrong. God could not find **10** people

there who loved him enough to do what was right.

 People even tried to harm angels God sent there!

 Angels came and led a man named Lot and his

family out of the city . The angel warned, " Do not

look back and do not stop ." Then the cities caught on

 fire and burned down to the ground ! Lot's wife did

not obey. She looked back, and she became salt!

What Did You Learn?

When you are following God,
keep looking forward.

A Mean Wedding Trick

Genesis 29:1-30

Jacob fell in love with a woman named Rachel who

took care of sheep. He worked **7** years for Rachel's

dad so he could marry Rachel. On their wedding

day, Jacob's bride wore a veil—a cloth that covered

her face. When the sun came up the next

morning, Jacob was surprised! His bride was not

Rachel! Her dad had tricked him! Jacob had mar-

ried the wrong woman, Rachel's sister, by mistake. Jacob

12

promised to work another **7** years so he could

marry Rachel.

What Did You Learn?

Be careful whom
you marry!

Joseph's Strange Dreams

Genesis 37:1-36;39:1—43:28

When Joseph was a boy, he had a . **11** ,

dream

stars

the , and the all bowed to him. God

sun

moon

down

told him the dream meant his whole family would

bow to him someday. When Joseph told his

down

family about his dream, they were very angry! But

many years later when Joseph lived in Egypt, the

Pharaoh

had a of **7** skinny eating **7** fat .

dream

cows

cows

Joseph told that during **7** years when

14

Pharaoh

food

wouldn't grow, 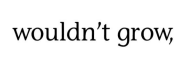 in would  the

people   Egypt   eat

 they had saved during **7** earlier years.

food   Pharaoh

then made Joseph a leader. And one day, Joseph's

family bowed to him, just like in his .

down   dream

What Did You Learn?

God knows what will happen
in the future.

Moses Sees God's Glory

Exodus 1:1—34:29

God did many miracles for Moses. He spoke from a burning bush, turned Moses'  staff into a snake, and made  Pharaoh let the Israelites follow Moses out of Egypt. God helped Moses split the sea and gave him water out of a rock to drink. 1 day Moses asked God to show his glory. God told him, "I will put you in an opening in a rock. I will cover you with my hand until I have passed by. Then I will remove my hand. You will see my back. But my face must not be seen."

What Did You Learn?

Have great respect
for the glory of God.

A Holdup Wins a Battle

Exodus 17:8-15

When an army attacked the  Israelites, Moses

stood on top of a hill with his staff in his  hands while

Joshua and some of the Israelites fought the

 army. As long as Moses held up his  hands, the

 Israelites won, but whenever he put down his hands,

they lost. When Moses' hands grew tired, he sat on a

 stone. Aaron and Hur held his hands up —1 on 1 side,

1 on the other—till the sun went down. That is how

the Israelites won the battle!

What Did You Learn?

We need to
help each other.

A House for God

Exodus 26-28; 1 Corinthians 6:19-20;
Hebrews 4:15-16; 6:19-20; 8:3-5, 9:11-14

God told the  to make a  called a

Israelites   tent

tabernacle where God would live. Later he had

Solomon build a to replace the tabernacle as

temple

God's home. The most holy room of the tabernacle

and held the that was like God's

temple   ark

throne in . Only the high priest could

heaven   go

into that room. was the last high priest. He

Jesus

made it so any **1** who believes in him can to
go

God's throne when we . In fact, God's Holy Spirit
pray

lives inside who believe in , so our
people   Jesus

bodies are now God's !
temple

What Did You Learn?

The tabernacle and temple were houses for God. Now our bodies are God's temple.

21

A Talking Donkey

Numbers 22:21-33

1 morning a named Balaam got angry and hit

man

his  for off the , for hurting

donkey   walking   road

Balaam's on a , and for lying . The

foot   wall   down

 talked! She said, "What have I done to make

donkey

you beat me?" The said, "You made a fool of me!"

man

He was angry that he couldn't make the .

donkey go

Then the saw that an was in the

man   angel

22

with a drawn. The was the rea-

road

sword

angel

son the had to 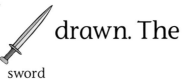 !

donkey

stop

What Did You Learn?

Sometimes angels are nearby and we don't even know.

A Spy Mission

Numbers 13:1-27

God wanted to give some land to the .

Israelites

Moses sent as spies to look at the land. He

men   go

said, "See whether the who live there are

people

 or weak, few or many. Is their land good or

strong

bad? Do their have ? Will the

cities   walls

 grow plants? Are there ? Do

ground   trees

your best to bring back some of the

fruit

land." They looked at the land for **40** days. **2** of the

24

came back carrying a huge bunch of

grapes on a pole between them. They told Moses

and the , "The land does flow with milk

and honey! Here is its ."

fruit

What Did You Learn?

God gives good gifts
to his children.

You Want to Go Where?

Numbers 13:28—14:34

God wanted the  Israelites to move into the good

land that the spies had seen. Caleb said, "We should

 go take the land!" The other spies said, "We can't.

We're not as strong as the giants there." That night

the  Israelites complained, "We should go back to

 Egypt ." Joshua said, " Do not rebel against God."

The people wanted to throw stones at Joshua

Moses, and Aaron! Then Moses saw a light , and

God said, "How long will they treat me like they

hate me? Why won't they believe in me?" Because

of his 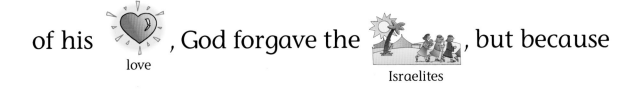, God forgave the , but because

they complained so much, they would have to

around lost in the for **40** years.

walk

desert

What Did You Learn?

Don't complain
about God's
plans.

Just Look and Live

Numbers 21:6-10, John 3:14-16

While the  Israelites were in the  desert,

 snakes bit them and many died. The  Israelites

asked Moses to pray. God told Moses to make a

bronze  snake and put it on a pole. When any **1**

who had been bitten by a  snake looked at the

bronze  snake, he lived. All the others died. The

 Bible says to lift up Jesus like Moses lifted the

28

bronze  so that any **1** who believes in

snake

 will live forever. God loved the so

Jesus

world

much that he gave his 1 and only Son that whoever

believes in will not die but will live forever.

Jesus

What Did You Learn?

If we show Jesus to people,
they can look to him and live.

29

Aaron's Staff Blooms

Numbers 1:50; 17:1-11

Some  **Israelites** didn't believe God put the Levites in

charge of the tabernacle. They were angry with

Moses and his brother Aaron. God told Moses, "Get **1**

❔**staff** from the leader of each of the **12** tribes and write

each man's name on his ❔**staff**." Aaron was from Levi's

tribe, so his name was on the Levite ❔**staff**. Moses said

that the staff belonging to the 🧍**man** God chose would

sprout. The very next day, Aaron's ❔**staff** not only sprout-

ed, but it budded, blossomed, and grew almond nuts!

30

What Did You Learn?

God cared about who was in charge of his tabernacle.

An Ark That Wasn't a Boat

Exodus 25:1-22 ; Deuteronomy 10 :55; Psalm 99:1 ; 1 Chronicles. 13:9-10;
Joshua 3:15-17; 1 Samuel 5:9-10; Hebrews 4:14-16; 9:4

Unlike Noah's ark , the ark in the temple was a

wooden box covered with gold. Its lid was called

"the mercy seat." It was like God's throne. Carved

 angels on the lid looked like those who worship

God in heaven . The ark held the 10 Commandments , some

manna, and Aaron's staff that bloomed. As Israelites

carried the ark into the Jordan River , the water

32

split so they could through on dry . Once
go   ground

when a man touched the , he died instantly.
ark

Another time, an  stole the and got
army   ark

lumps under their skin. They quickly gave the ark

back to the . Solomon put the in the
Israelites   ark

holiest room of the .
temple

What Did You Learn?

The ark
reminded the
Israelites
that God was
with them.

Joshua's Amazing Battles

Joshua 1:1—24:24

God made the (river) (stop) so Joshua could lead the

 (Israelites) across on dry (ground) into Canaan. God

promised, "I will give you every place where you set

your (foot)." Remember how God made a (wall)

fall (down) and how he made the (sun) (stop) so

Joshua's (army)

could win battles

for the Promised

Land? When a

bad tried to run away from Joshua, God

sent big hailstones from the ! The

hailstones killed more of the bad than the

 of the  did! Joshua reminded his

, "It was God who fought for you." He got

them to promise that they would serve and obey

God. He gave each  family part of the

Promised Land.

What Did You Learn?

God gives what he promises.

The Moldy Bread Trick

Joshua 9

To get the Israelites to promise not to fight them, the

Gibeonites pretended to live farther away than

they really did. They loaded  donkeys with worn-

out sacks, put patched sandals on their 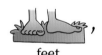 feet,

wore old clothes, and brought bread that was

dry and green with mold to Joshua. They lied and

said these had all been new when they began their

trip. The  Israelites did not pray about what to do.

They wrote down a promise that they would not

fight the Gibeonites. When they learned about the

trick, they didn't fight. Instead, they used the

Gibeonites for  .

servants

What Did You Learn?

We need to pray
before we make
decisions.

Amazing Deborah Wins a War

Judges 4

A **woman** named Deborah was an  **Israelite** leader. She

decided who was **right** and who was **wrong**. **1** day

she told Barak, "God says to take an  **army** to a

 mountain where God will put the other army's leader

into your **hands**."Barak would not **go** without

Deborah. She said, "I will **go** with you, but if you

 do not do this the way God said, the honor will not

be yours. God will hand that leader to a ."

woman

Deborah's and Barak's  won, but a

army   woman

named Jael, instead of Barak, was the **1** who killed

the other army's leader.

What Did You Learn?

It would be a shame if we didn't obey God
and he had to use someone else.

Surprising Signs for Gideon

Judges 6

An  told Gideon to lead the  in a

angel   Israelites

battle. Gideon wanted to be sure this was what God

wanted and that God would help him. Gideon said to

God, "I will place a fleece outside. If there is dew only

on the fleece and all the is dry, I will know

ground

that you will save the ." The next morning

Israelites

the fleece was wet and the was dry! Gideon

ground

, "Let me ask for **1** more test. This time make

prayed

40

the fleece dry and the covered with dew."

ground

The next morning the fleece was dry and the

 was wet!

ground

What Did You Learn?

It is important that we try to find
God's will for our lives.

The Incredible Shrinking Army

Judges 7:1-22

God wanted the army men to know that when

they won a battle it was through his help, not just

because they had many strong men. God told

Gideon to send home any **1** in the  army who was

 afraid to fight. Then he told Gideon to take the men

who were left to get a drink at the river. God told

Gideon to send home the men who got down on

their knees to drink water. Gideon only kept **300**

who lapped with their to their mouths.

men

hands

Then God told Gideon's small how to win.

army

They blew trumpets, broke , held torches,

jars

and shouted. The other  fought themselves

army

by mistake, , and ran away!

cried

What Did You Learn?

God is our strength.

Samuel Picks the Little Guy

1 Samuel 16:1-13

Samuel had to find out which of Jesse's sons God

wanted to be 👑 king . God said, " ⊘ Do not think about how

he looks or how tall he is. 🧍 Man looks at the outside, but

God looks at the ❤️ heart ." Samuel met **7** of Jesse's sons

and knew God had not chosen any of them. Then

Jesse said his youngest son was taking care of 🐑 sheep .

That 🧕 shepherd was David. He was the **1** God wanted. So

Samuel put drops of oil on David to show that he

would be 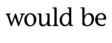 . Later David fought a and won.

Then after many years, he became .

What Did You Learn?

God looks at the heart.

Saul's Close Calls

1 Samuel 24; 26:5-25 ; 1 Chronicles 10:4-14

1 day while David was playing the harp for King

Saul, Saul threw a spear at David! David ran away.

For a long time, King Saul and his army chased

David and planned to kill him. **1** time Saul came

into a cave and didn't see David in the dark.

David cut off a corner of Saul's coat to prove to

Saul that he had passed up a chance to kill him.

Later David found Saul asleep with his spear stuck in

the ground near his head. He took the spear to prove

he had shown mercy to Saul again. Later  Saul

died, and David became the .

What Did You Learn?

God doesn't want us to take revenge.

David Helps a Lame Guy

2 Samuel 9

 Saul's son, Jonathan, was David's very close friend. After Saul and Jonathan died, David became . He asked, "Is any **1** left in Saul's family to whom I can show kindness for Jonathan's sake?" A 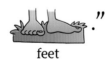 said, "Jonathan's son is alive. He is crippled in both feet." David gave the lame son land and after that always let him eat at his table like **1** of his sons. The lame man asked,

48

"Why should you notice a dead like me?"

dog   King

David showed kindness like God does. We're like the

 who felt as worthless as a dead . God wants us

man   dog

at his in as his !

table   heaven   children

What Did You Learn?

Show kindness like God does.

49

Who's the Real Mom?

1 Kings 3:16-28

 King Solomon asked God for wisdom, and God gave

it. **1** day **2** **women** came to see **King** Solomon. They

both said they were **1** baby's mother. The **king**

pretended he thought the **baby** should be cut in **2**

pieces so half of the **baby** could go to each **woman**. The

real mom **loved** her **baby**. She said, "Give the **baby**

to her! Don't kill him!" Then the **king** knew who

the real mom was. He let the **baby** live, and gave

50

him to the who wanted him to be safe. The

woman

 saw that the had wisdom from God

Israelites king

to do what was and fair.

right

What Did You Learn?

Wisdom comes from God.

51

 The Incredible Expanding Food

1 Kings 17:1-16

During a time when no fell for years, there

rain

was not much or . God sent **black**

food   water

 to bring and meat to Elijah **2**

birds   bread

times each day. Then God told a to share with

woman

him. When Elijah asked her for a of

drink   water

and a piece of , she told him, "I only have

bread

a little flour and oil." She thought the flour and oil

would make her last meal for her son and herself

before they starved. The 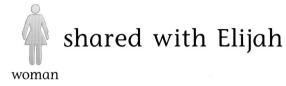 shared with Elijah

woman

anyway, and the flour and oil did not run out until

God sent  .

rain

What Did You Learn?

God blesses us when we do what he asks.

Fire Falls from Heaven

1 Kings 18:16-40

Elijah said to who a , "You offer meat to

people   worshiped   statue

your god. I'll offer meat to my God. The god who catches the

meat on is real." The   to the , but no **1**

fire   people   prayed   statue

answered. Elijah teased, "Maybe he is asleep." Then Elijah

prayed

to the real God, "I did what you said. Answer me so these

people

will know you're God and you're turning their back

hearts

again." Then came and burned the meat, the

fire   down   up

wood, and even around it! The fell and ,

water   people   down   cried

"The Lord is God!"

54

What Did You Learn?

God wants people
to know he is real.

Three Thirsty Kings

2 Kings 3

After **3** kings marched for **7** days with their army, they had no more water for themselves or their animals. **1** king asked

Elisha for help. Elisha told him, "God says to make

this valley full of ditches. You will see neither

 nor , yet this valley will be filled
wind   rain

with . You, your , and your other
water   cows

 will . This is easy in the of the
animals   drink   eyes

Lord. You will win your battle, too." The next morn-

ing flowing filled the valley. Then the **3**
water

 won the battle just as God said they would.
kings

What Did You Learn?

Amazing miracles are easy for the Lord.

The Miraculous Oil Jar

2 Kings 4:1-7

A could not repay she owed to some

woman · money

. They wanted to take her sons and make

people

them work as . She turned to Elisha for help.

servants

He asked, "What do you have in your ?" She

house

said, "Just a little oil." Elisha said, " ask neighbors

Go

for empty . Ask for many. Then inside,

jars · go

shut the , and pour oil into all the ."

door · jars

The of oil kept pouring until there were no

jar

58

left to fill. Then the oil stopped flowing.

Elisha said, ", sell the oil, and pay the you

owe. You and your sons can live on the that

is left."

What Did You Learn?

We can trust God to take care of us.

2 Kings 6:1-7

A 🧍 **man** named Elisha listened to God. He and his

friends wanted to build a meeting place near the

Jordan 🏞️ **River**, so they got to work. They chopped

⬇️ **down** 🌳 **trees** with an 🪓 **axe**. As **1** 🧍 **man** was cutting ⬇️ **down**

a 🌳 **tree**, the metal part of the 🪓 **axe** fell into the

🌊 **water** and sank. "Oh no!" he 😢 **cried** out, "I had

borrowed that 🪓 **axe**!" Elisha cut a stick and threw it

where the 🪓 **axe** head had fallen. That made the

heavy metal part of the axe float! "Lift it out,"

Elisha said. Then the man reached out his 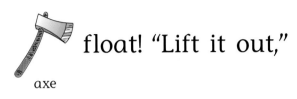 hand and

took it.

What Did You Learn?

God even cares about our little problems.

Chariots of Fire to the Rescue

2 Kings 6:8-23

When Elisha's servant got up **1** morning, he saw an evil king's

 army , horses , and chariots around the city . The

 servant was afraid . Elisha prayed, "O Lord, open his eyes so he

may see." Then the servant saw the hills full of horses and

 chariots made of fire all around! As the bad army

came toward him, Elisha prayed , "Strike them blind." The

 army could not see! Elisha led them to another city .

Then when he asked God to open their eyes , they could see

again. Elisha let the army go back to their king .

62

What Did You Learn?

Sometimes we can't see
all of the help God has sent.

An Eight-Year-Old King

2 Kings 22:1—23:30

Josiah was **8** years old when he became . He

king

did what was . He had workers fix the  .

right   temple

They found part of the that no **1** had read

Bible

for a long time. Josiah felt that his

King   sad   people

had not obeyed what the  said. Josi-

Bible   King

ah told God he was sorry, and he . Because the

cried

  , God put a to his plans to destroy

king   prayed   stop

their land. Josiah read the  aloud to his

King   Bible

people

. They promised to follow God and keep his

commands with all of their and soul.

heart

What Did You Learn?

A leader who loves
God can turn his
people away
from evil.

A Shadow Creeps Backward

2 Kings 20:1-11, 20

A  named Hezekiah got . Isaiah told him,

"The Lord says to get ready because you will die."

Hezekiah and . After Isaiah left the palace,

God sent him back to tell the that God said, "I

heard you and saw you . I will heal you. I

will add **15** years to your life. And I will not let the

 of Assyria rule over you." Hezekiah asked how

he could be sure. Isaiah for the shadow on the

66

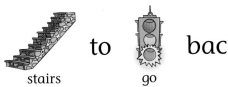 to  backwards up the **10**  it

stairs   go   stairs

had already gone ⬇, and that's what happened!

down

What Did You Learn?

God is in charge of how long we live.

A Praying Queen Foils a Plot

Esther 1-10

A bad man named Haman got a king to say that all

the Jews would be killed. The king did not know

that his wife, a queen named Esther, was Jewish.

 Queen Esther wanted to stop Haman's evil plan, but a

 queen could be killed if she went to see the king when

he had not called for her. Her uncle said to her, "Who

knows, but maybe you have become the queen for

such a time as this?" Queen Esther asked the Jews to

fast—not or —for **3** days. After **3** days,

eat   drink

 Esther went to see the . He was glad to see

Queen   king

her! The let the Jews live. He had bad Haman

king

killed instead.

What Did You Learn?

It is good to pray and
fast with friends about
big problems.

It Couldn't Get Much Worse

Job 1—42

A **man** named Job **prayed** often and did **right**. God let

Satan tempt Job. **Fire** killed his **sheep** and **servants**.

His **camels** were stolen. **Wind** blew **down** a **house**,

killing his **children**. Job bowed to the **ground** in

 **worship**. He said, "The Lord gave and the Lord has

taken away." Then sores covered Job, but Job didn't

sin. He said, "Should we take good from God, and not

trouble?" Friends said he must have sinned to

70

deserve all this. God said Job's friends were  . He

wrong

gave Job twice what he had before.

What Did You Learn?

Trust God even in hard times,
and don't blame people
when bad things happen to them.

New Testament

Christmas Angels

Luke 1:26-39; Matthew 1:18-21

1 day an surprised a young named
angel · woman

Mary. He said, " You will have a . Name him
baby

 ." The explained, "He will be the Son
Jesus · angel

of God. Nothing is impossible with God." An
angel

came to Joseph, the who was engaged to Mary.
man

The said in a , " be to take
angel · dream · Do not · afraid

Mary as your wife. Name the Jesus because he
baby

will save from their sins." When was
people · baby Jesus

74

born, an angel said to some shepherds, "A Savior has

been born to you! He is Christ the Lord. Suddenly

a large group of  angels from  heaven also

appeared and praised God!

What Did You Learn?

Jesus is the Son of God,
and he saves us
from our sins.

God Speaks Up for His Son

Matthew 17:1-8; 3:16-17; John 12:20-28

God spoke from  the day Jesus was
heaven

baptized and said, "This is my Son, whom I ;
love

I am well pleased with him." God said the same

thing from a while and **3** friends
cloud   Jesus

were on a . That day God added, "Listen to
mountain

him!" Jesus' friends were so , they fell on the
afraid   down

 . On another day, told friends he
ground   Jesus

would die on the soon and receive glory. He
cross

76

said, "Father, glorify your name!" A voice from

 said, "I have glorified it, and will glorify it

heaven

again."

What Did You Learn?

God loves his Son Jesus and is pleased
with him. He wants us to listen to him.

Jesus Heals Ten Men at Once

Matthew 9:20-22, 2-30; 8:14-15; Mark 2:1-12;
Luke 5:12-13, 6:6-10; 17:11-19; 22:49-51

One day 10 **men** with a skin disease called loudly, "**Jesus**, Master, have pity on us!" Jesus said, "**Go** show yourself to the religious leaders." And as they went, Jesus made their skin disease disappear! One **man** came back praising God loudly. He threw himself at the **feet** of **Jesus** and thanked him. Jesus asked, "Weren't all **10** cleansed? Where are the other **9**?

Then he said to the **man**, "Get **up** and **go**; your faith has made you well." **Jesus** healed the **eyes** of blind men. He helped lame men to walk . Jesus touched

the hand of a woman with a fever and the fever left.

 Jesus said to a man whose hand was shriveled, "Stretch

out your hand ." He did and his hand was normal!

What Did You Learn?

Jesus cares when we're sick, and he wants us to thank him when he heals us.

Back to Life

Luke 7:11-17; 8:49—9:1, John 11:1-46

 brought some back to life after they

people

died. When he saw a dead carried out of the

man

, Jesus felt for the man's mom and said

city · sad

to her, "Don't ." told the dead to get .

cry · Jesus · man · up

The sat and began talking! After a 12-year-

man · up

old died, Jesus took her and said, "My child,

girl · hand

get !" She did! After Lazarus had been in a

up

 for **4** days, said to the man's sister, "I

tomb · Jesus

am the resurrection and the life. Whoever believes

in me will live, even though he dies." After the stone

was moved from the doorway of the  tomb Jesus

called to the dead man, "Lazarus, come out!" Every

1 was amazed when Lazarus  walked out of

the  tomb.

What Did You Learn?

Jesus has power over
life and death.

Jesus—A Good Friend to Bad People

Matthew 9:9-13; Mark 2:13-17;
Luke 5:27-32; John 8:1-11; Luke 7:36-50

1 time 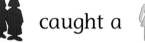 caught a doing . They brought her to

people · woman · wrong

 and wanted to throw at her. said, "If any

Jesus · stones · Jesus

of you is without sin, let him be the first to throw a ."

stone

Every **1** left except the and . He told her, "I

woman · Jesus · do not

want you to be punished. and leave your life of sin."

Go

Another day a who had been sinful came to . She

woman · Jesus

 on his and wiped them with her . Jesus said,

cried · feet · hair

"Her many sins have been forgiven because she much.

loved

But he who has been forgiven little little."

loves

82

What Did You Learn?

Jesus loves us even
when we have
done wrong.

Love Your Enemies

Matthew 5:44-48; 22:37-40; John 13:34, 35

 Jesus said loving God and other people are the

greatest commands. Every command in the

 Bible is about showing love . Jesus said to

even love your enemies and pray for those who

are mean to you. After all, God makes his sun rise

on both the evil and the good,

and he sends rain on both

those who do right and those

who do **wrong**. We are not just supposed to **love**

those who **love** us or only say hello to friends and

family. Even **people** without God do that.  **Jesus**

said, "As I have loved you, so you must **love**

1 another. This is how all men will know that you

learn from me, if you **love** **1** another."

What Did You Learn?

God wants us to love everyone
like he does.

What Is Most Valuable

Matthew 19:16-26; 13:45-46

 Jesus said, "The kingdom of heaven is like a sales-

man who looked for fine pearls. When he found **1** of

great value, he sold everything he had and bought

the pearl." The kingdom of God was worth more

than what the man gave up for it. Jesus asked a

young ruler who had a lot of money to sell all he had

and give to the poor so he would have treasure in

 heaven . Instead the man went away sad . He made

the  choice. Disciples of made the

wrong

Jesus

right

choice. They even away

walked

from their jobs to follow .

Jesus

What Did You Learn?

Following Jesus as King is worth more than anything.

87

How Many Hairs Do You Have?

Matthew 6:25-30; 10:28-3; Luke 15:3-24; James 4:8

You matter very much to God. said that if **1**
Jesus

 falls to the , God knows about it.
bird   ground

And you are worth more than the . He
birds

said even the hairs of your head are counted! God

feeds the and clothes the , so you
birds   flowers

can trust him to feed and clothe you. If you ever

wandered away from God, he would look for

you like a looks for his lost . told
shepherd   sheep   Jesus

88

about a runaway son who did things. The son
wrong

wanted to come home, but he was his dad
afraid

would be very . Instead, the dad ran out to hug
mad

him! God feels that

way about you!

What Did You Learn?

We matter very much to God!

89

Peter Starts to Walk by Faith

Matthew 8:23-27; 14:22-33; 15:32-38; Luke 5:1-11; John 21:1-14

 Jesus did many miracles. He fed thousands of people with only

1 boy's lunch. He filled nets with fish . He even calmed a

 storm instantly! On another night , Jesus walked on water

across the sea to friends who were on a boat . Peter wanted to

 walk on the sea, too. When Jesus said to him, "Come," Peter

did. But as soon as Peter saw the wind , he became afraid and

began to sink. Peter cried , "Lord, save me!" Jesus caught him by

the hand and said, "You of little faith, why did you doubt?"

When they climbed into the boat , the people in the boat

worshiped Jesus saying, "Truly you are the Son of God."

90

What Did You Learn?

Jesus can do what seems impossible, so walk by faith and don't let doubts pull you down.

Runaway Pigs

Mark 5:1-20

A lived among . No **1** was

man   tombs   strong

enough to control him. He broke chains, out,

cried

and cut himself with . When he saw ,

stones   Jesus

he fell on his knees and shouted, "What do you

want with me, , Son of God?" said,

Jesus   Jesus

"Come out of him, you evil spirit!" The many evil

spirits that were in the man went out of him and

into a herd of about **2,000** . The

pigs   pigs

rushed  the hill into the lake and drowned.

down

Now the ⋔ was fine. Jesus said, "🚦 tell your

man   Go

family how much the Lord has done for you."

What Did You Learn?

Jesus is stronger than evil.

93

A Fish Delivers a Coin

Matthew 17:24-27

Where lived, paid called taxes

Jesus   people   money

to take care of the and its workers. Someone

temple

asked Peter, "Doesn't pay the tax?"

Jesus   temple

Peter said, "Yes, he does." When Peter came into the

, was the first to speak. He asked, "Do

house   Jesus

 of the collect

kings   world

taxes from their

own sons or

others?" Peter said, "From others." "Then the sons

 have to pay," said. "But so that we may

do not   Jesus

not upset them, to the lake and throw your line

go

into the . Take the first you catch;

water   fish

open its mouth and you will find a coin. Give it to

them for our tax."

What Did You Learn?

God can give us what we need...
even in unusual ways.

#

Luke 22:39-54

Jesus went to a to . He wanted to be

mountain   pray

ready for the time when he would die on a .

cross

After , a mob showed up who wanted to

Jesus   prayed

take him away. Jesus' friend Peter wanted to

stop

them. He lifted a and cut off the right of a

sword   ear

 named Malchus. Jesus said, "No more of this!"

servant

He touched the man's and healed him.

ear

What Did You Learn?

Jesus even helped people
who wanted to harm him.

97

 The Day Jesus Died

Matthew 27:50-61; Mark 15:37-16:1;
Luke 23:44-56; John 19:38-42

When **Jesus** died on the **cross** , many amazing

events happened. The **sun** stopped shining. The

 temple curtain, which had separated **people** from

God, tore apart. The **ground** shook,  **rocks** split

and 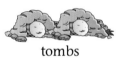 **tombs** broke open. After Jesus rose, bodies

of holy **people** who had died came to life and went

into the **city** ! When the guards saw the

earthquake and all that happened, they were **afraid**

and said, "Surely was the Son of God!" Joseph

Jesus

of Arimathea took the body of  from

Jesus down

the . With the help of a 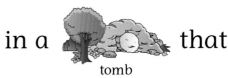 named Nicodemus,

cross man

Joseph put the body of in a  that

Jesus tomb

had never been used.

What Did You Learn?

Surely Jesus is the Son of God.

99

Jesus Appears

Luke 24:13-53

While **2** men were on the road to Emmaus,

 Jesus began to walk with them. They didn't

recognize him. They told him, "Our rulers put

 Jesus on a cross **3** days ago. Women went to the

 tomb, but didn't find his body. They told us

 angels said he was alive. Our friends went to the

 tomb but they did not see  Jesus."  Jesus said,

"You are slow to believe all the  says! Christ

Bible

had to suffer these things." Then the invited

men

Jesus into their . **He** sat at their , ,

house   table   prayed

and handed them some . That's when they

bread

saw that he was , and he disappeared! Many

Jesus

others saw alive, too.

Jesus

What Did You Learn?

Jesus is alive! He did what the Bible said
he would do.

The Sewing Lady Comes Back

Acts 9:36-41

A named Tabitha sewed clothes for a living. She

woman

did good and helped who didn't have

people

enough . **1** day Tabitha became and died.

money   sick

Some who followed said to Peter,

people   Jesus

"Please come at once!" When Peter went into the

room where Tabitha's body was, he saw .

women   crying

They showed him the clothes Tabitha had made

while she was still alive. Peter sent them out. Then he

got on his knees to . He turned toward the

dead and said, "Tabitha, get ." She opened her

 and sat ! Peter took her and helped

her to her . Many in the

heard about this and believed in .

What Did You Learn?

When people hear about the
great things God has done,
many believe in him.

Two Liars Drop Dead

Acts 4:32—5:12

After (Jesus) went to (heaven), his followers shared

all they had. No **1** was needy, because from time to

time, (people) who sold their land or (houses) brought

the (money) to the apostles. Then those leaders gave

the (money) to whoever had a need. Ananias and his

wife, Sapphira, sold some land, but kept part of the

 (money). Then they brought the rest to the leaders as if

it was all of the (money). Peter said, "You have not lied

to men but to God." Ananias fell dead.

down   Men

carried him out and buried him. His wife came in

later and lied, too. Peter said, "The of the

feet

 who buried your husband are at the .

men   door

They will carry you out also." Then she fell at his

down

 dead. buried her beside her husband.

feet   Men

What Did You Learn?

God knows the truth.

Angel Power Opens a Gate

Acts 12:1-17

 King Herod put Peter in jail for telling people about Jesus.

The people of the church began to pray for Peter. While Peter

was asleep and chained between **2** soldiers, an angel came.

The angel woke him. "Quick, get up!" he said. The chains fell

off Peter's wrists. Then the angel told him to put on clothes

and follow him. Peter followed the angel out of jail. The

gate leading to the city opened by itself. Then the angel

left. Peter went to a house where many people were praying. He

told them how God had brought him out of jail.

What Did You Learn?

God can lead us out of our problems.

 Philip Disappears!

Acts 8:26-9:1-40

An **angel** told Philip to **walk** **down** a **road**

through the  **desert**. There he saw an African **man**

riding a  **chariot**. The Spirit told Philip, " **Go** to

that **chariot**." Philip ran to it and heard the **man**

reading the **Bible**. "Do you understand it?"

Philip asked. The **man** said, "I need someone to

explain it." He asked Philip to sit with him. Philip

said the verse was about **Jesus**. When they came

to some  near the , the asked Philip

water   road   man

to baptize him. When they came out of the

up

, Philip was suddenly gone! Philip showed

water

in another and told there

up   city   people

about .

Jesus

What Did You Learn?

God can put us in the right place
at the right time to tell about Jesus.

109

Stephen Sees Right into Heaven

Acts 6:1—8:3

Stephen helped the church give food to widows.

Stephen told people all about the Bible. He said

their families killed Bible prophets who said

 Jesus would come. He said these people themselves

had killed Jesus They were very angry! Stephen

looked up to heaven and saw the glory of God, and

 Jesus standing at the right hand of God. The people

threw rocks. Stephen prayed, "Lord Jesus, receive my

spirit. Do not hold this sin against them." After he

said that, he died and went to Heaven.

110

What Did You Learn?

Jesus is with us as we bravely tell others about him.

111

A Clever Escape

Acts 9:20-25

Saul, who was also called Paul, was cruel to Christians. Then **1** day a light blinded him. **H**e heard speak and believed in . After God healed his , Saul began to preach that is the Son of God. who heard him were amazed. They asked, "Isn't he the who caused trouble for Christians? Has he come here to take them to ?" Yet Saul proved to them that

Jesus

Jesus

Jesus

eyes

People

man

jail

Jesus is the Christ. Some  people plotted to kill Saul,

but he learned of their plan. Day and night they kept

close watch on the gates of the city so they could

kill him as he came out. But one night his friends

lowered him in a basket through

an opening in the wall of

the city .

What Did You Learn?

Tell others about Jesus
even if it's risky.

113

An Earthquake Shakes the Jail

Acts 16:16-40

Paul and Silas were beaten and thrown into .
jail

Instead of crying, they prayed and sang hymns to God!

An earthquake shook the jail. The doors flew open,

and everybody's chains came loose. The jailer was

afraid he would be in big trouble if prisoners escaped.

Paul shouted, "We are all here!" The jailer fell down in

front of Paul and Silas. He asked, "What must I do to

be saved?" They said, "Believe in the Lord Jesus, and

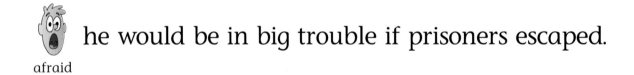

114

you will be saved." The jailer and his family were bap-

tized. He was very happy his whole family believed in

God. In the morning, leaders told him to let Paul and

Silas  go free.

What Did You Learn?

Praise God in every situation.
He can turn what's bad
into good.

Falling Out the Window

Acts 20:7-12

One night people who believed in Jesus had a

meeting. A young man named Eutychus sat in a third-

story window listening to Paul talk. Paul talked for a

long, long time until midnight. The young man's

 eyes began to close. He sank into a deep sleep and

fell out the window down to the ground. When they

picked him up, he was dead! Paul went down the

 stairs, threw himself on the young man and put his

arms around him. "Don't be ," he said. "He's
afraid

alive!" They were that Eutychus was alive. Then
happy

they all went back the  , ate ,
up   stairs   bread

and listened to Paul talk until the rose.
sun

What Did You Learn?

God can do great things through
people who trust him.

117

Shipwrecked!

Acts 27

While Paul was in jail, he and other prisoners

had to go to Italy by boat. A terrible storm arose. The

 people were afraid. Paul said to them, "An angel told me

not **1** of you will be lost; only the boat will be

destroyed." The boat ran into a sandbar, and the

back part of the boat was broken to pieces by the

waves. Some men jumped into the water to swim to

land. The rest got there on wooden planks or pieces

of the boat. Everyone was safe!

What Did You Learn?

When we're in danger,
we can trust God.

119

After the shipwreck, Paul and the others swam or

floated to shore in the cold . The nice

rain   people

on the island built a . As Paul put wood on

fire

the , a poisonous  came out of the

fire   snake

wood and bit Paul! When the saw the

people

 hanging from Paul's , they thought

snake   hand

Paul was being punished for doing something

 . But Paul just shook the  off into the

wrong   snake

fire . Paul did not swell **up** or die. He was fine.

Then **people** thought he was a god. Of course, Paul was not a god, and the people should have

 **worshiped** the real God who saved him instead!

What Did You Learn?

The devil attacks us when we're down,
but God helps us survive.

God's Amazing Grace

John 3:16; 23-25; 14:6-7; Romans 5:8;
Ephesians 2:8-10; 1 John 2:3-6, 9-10

God's grace is the undeserved kindness he shows us.

Because God us, he offers us a way to
loves

 . Jesus said, "I am the way.... No **1** comes to
heaven

the Father except through me." We sin when we do

 things and also when we do what is
wrong   do not

good and . Sin could have kept us out of
right

 . But because of his grace, God let
heaven   Jesus

take punishment for our sins on the . God
cross

122

 the so much that he gave his **1** and

loved   world

only Son so whoever believes in will not die

Jesus

but will live forever in  .

heaven

What Did You Learn?

Because of God's amazing grace,
he sent Jesus to be the way
for us to go to heaven.

Dressed in Armor

Ephesians 6:10-17

Be strong in the Lord and put on the full armor of God

so you can stand against the devil's tricks. We don't

fight against people but against evil. Believe and tell

the truth—buckle the belt of truth around your

waist. Be right with God through 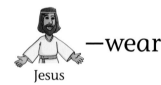 Jesus —wear

the breastplate of righteousness. Be ready to share

good news about peace that Jesus gives—put on

readiness shoes. Believe God—hold a shield of faith

against temptations the devil shoots like fiery

arrows. Trust to save you—wear a of

Jesus   helmet

salvation. Remember the Word of God—fight the

devil with the [sword] of the Spirit.

What Did You Learn?

Be strong in the Lord
    so we're ready
to fight temptations.

We're the Body of Christ

1 Corinthians 12; Ephesians 4:1-16

God gives his Holy Spirit to people who believe in

 Jesus . The Holy Spirit gives us the power to serve

God. Just like 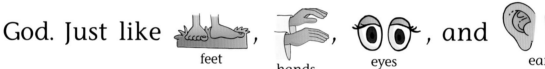 feet , hands , eyes , and ears

work together in a body, believers with different

abilities work together for Jesus. The eye can't say to

the hand , "I don't need you!" Christians need each

other very much. If **1** part suffers, every part suffers

with it. If **1** part is honored, every part is happy with

126

it. Every believer is an important part of the body

of Christ, and Jesus is the head. As each part does its

work, the body grows in .

love

What Did You Learn?

Christians need to work together
like parts of a body.

We're Going Up in the Air

Matthew 24:36-44; 25:1-30; Mark 13:32-37;
Luke 12:35-56; 21:34-36; 1 Thessalonians 4:16-18

When went to in the ,

 told the there that would return

the same way. said he will come back when no **1**

expects him. Even the 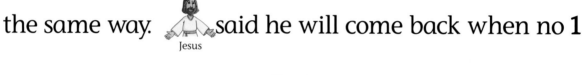 know the exact

day or hour. A will sound when comes

 from .  who died believing in him will

rise first. After that, believers who are still alive will

catch with them in the to meet  in

the air and to be with forever!

What Did You Learn?

Jesus wants us to be ready
for his return.

Subject Index

10 Commandments . . 32

A

Aaron 18, 26, 30
Abraham 8
Adam and Eve 2
Angels 8, 10, 22, 32,
40, 74, 100, 106,
108, 118, 128
Animals 4, 57, 88, 92
Ark of the
Covenant 20, 32
Armor of God 124

B

Babies 8, 50, 74
Baptize 109, 115
Believing God 27, 103,
124
Believing in Jesus . . .21, 29,
103, 112, 114,
116, 128

Bible 64, 84, 101,
108, 110
Birds 52, 88
Body of Christ 127

C

Caleb 26
Canaan 34
Christians 112, 126
Cross 76, 96, 98, 122

D

David 44, 46, 48
Deborah 38
Devil 121, 124
Dreams 14

E

Elijah 52, 54
Elisha . . .57, 58, 60, 62, 64
Esther 68

F

Faith 78, 90, 124
Fasting 69
Fire 10, 54, 120
Following Jesus 87
Forgiveness 3, 82
Fruit 24

G

Garden of Eden 2
Gideon 40, 42
Giving thanks 78
Glory of God . .16, 76, 110
God's will 40
Grace 122

H

Heaven . . .3, 6, 49, 76, 110,
123, 128
Helping People 19
Hezekiah 66
High Priest 20
Holy Spirit 21, 126
Humility 7

I

Isaiah 66
Israelites 16, 18, 20,
24, 26, 27, 28, 30,
33, 34, 35, 36, 38, 40

J

Jacob 12
Jesus example 84
Jesus heals 78, 96
Jesus Saves 74
Jesus Returns 128
Job 70
Jonathan 48
Joseph 14
Joshua 18, 26, 34
Josiah 64

K

Kindness 49
Kingdom of Heaven . . .86

L

Lazarus 80, 81
Lies 105

Lot 10
Love 82, 84, 127

M

Mary 74
Miracles 8, 16, 30, 34,
   57, 60, 78, 80, 90
Moses 16, 18, 24, 26, 28, 30

N

Noah 4

O

Obeying God . . .10, 39, 42
Oil 44, 52, 58

P

Paul . . .112, 114, 116, 118, 120
Pearls 86
Peter 90, 94, 96,
   102, 104, 106
Pharaoh 14, 16
Philip 108
Prayer 36, 37, 54, 62,
   66, 70, 96, 103, 106,
Pride 6

Promises 4, 35, 36, 65
Prophets 110

R

Rachel 12
Resurrection 80

S

Salvation 29
Samuel 44
Satan 70
Sarah 8
Saul 46
Sharing 52
Sheep 44, 88
Sin 2, 82, 110, 122
Snakes 16, 28, 120
Solomon 20, 50
Son of God 75, 76, 90,
   92, 99, 112
Stephen 110
Sword 23, 35, 96

T

Tabernacle 20, 31

Taxes 94

Temple 20, 33, 64, 94

Tombs 80, 92, 98, 100

Tower of Babel 6, 7

Trust God 59

Trusting God . . .58, 117, 119

W

Wedding 12

Wisdom 50, 51

Who Is Jesus?

QUESTION: Who is Jesus?
ANSWER: Jesus is God's Son.

Because sin came into the world when Adam and Eve disobeyed God, God asked Jesus to come to make things right again.

Jesus was born (just about 2,000 years ago), and he lived in a part of the world called Palestine.

When he was about thirty years old, he began to preach and to heal.

Three or four years later he was nailed to a cross to die. When the people who loved him went to his grave three days later, Jesus' body wasn't there.

He had come back to life, just as he said he would.

QUESTION: Where is Jesus now?
ANSWER: Jesus is in heaven with his Father.

But he has not left us alone here on earth. He sent the Holy Spirit to live with us—to make us strong when we feel like giving up,
> to help us to care about other people
> when we sometimes don't feel like it,
> to tell us that Jesus will always love us.

QUESTION: Why did Jesus have to die?
ANSWER: It was all part of God's great plan to make right what had become so wrong because of sin.

You see, we all deserve to be punished.

God loves us so much he sent Jesus to take our punishment. Because of Jesus we can know for sure that God welcomes us into his loving arms—right now and when we die and go to be with him.

QUESTION: Does Jesus love me?
ANSWER: Jesus loves you more than you can imagine.

He loves you when you cry and when you laugh; when you argue with your brother or when you've had a bad day. He loves you so much that he died for you—but he isn't still dead. He is alive, and he is loving and watching over you every day.

QUESTION: Will Jesus ever stop loving me?
ANSWER: No!

There will be times when you wonder if Jesus is really real.

There will be times when you wonder if he loves you. There will be times when you do things that you shouldn't— when you act mean to your sister or lie to your father.

But when you pray and tell Jesus that you have times when you doubt; when you pray and tell Jesus that you know you've done wrong and you want to do better— you can be sure that he will never let you down.

He will love you your whole life long, and you will live with him forever.

QUESTION: How do I know I'm a Christian?
ANSWER: There are many signs.

When you love Jesus with all the love you can give, when you know deep down that Jesus loves you, when you believe he died to forgive your sins, when you want to live for Jesus—those are good signs that help you know you are a Christian.

Sure, you're going to fail sometimes. But, you see, God's love for you is so great that it covers those times when you fail. He sees deep into your heart. He knows your desire to live for him, and *he loves you.*